The Sun's Shadow:

An Anthology of Love and Longing

Ernest Roberson Sr

Trient Press
3375 S Rainbow Blvd
#81710, SMB 13135
Las Vegas,NV 89180

Ordering Information:
Quantity sales. Special discounts are available on quantity purchases by corporations, associations, and others. For details, contact the publisher at the address above.
Orders by U.S. trade bookstores and wholesalers. Please contact Trient Press: Tel: (775) 996-3844; or visit www.trientpress.com.

Printed in the United States of America

Publisher's Cataloging-in-Publication data
Roberson Sr, Ernest
A title of a book : The Sun's Shadow: An Anthology of Love and Longing

ISBN
Hard Cover 979-8-88990-010-8
Paper Back 979-8-88990-011-5
Ebook 979-8-88990-012-2

Dedication

For my three children, Jersey Lynn, Ernest Jr. and Aaron Columbus, who shines on.

Also For..................

Annika Akesdotter, Stacy Nicholson and Sheena Davis, for contributing or being my inspiration within these words.

The More Loving One

Her shine, I should say,
could take me anywhere.
She walks in beauty,
like the night.
A spirit beautiful and bright.
I loved and guessed at you.
Yet loved me for what might,
or might not be.
Perhaps you saw too,
that feeling would stay.
I carry your heart with me.
I'm never without it.
Let the more loving one be me.
If ever two were one,
then it's surely we.

Touched My Life

I don't think you'll fully understand how you touched my life.
You gave me light to my soul.
Helped me to be whole.
I'll never forget knowing your smile.
I came to realize that you're always on my mind.
I never stop thinking about you.
I promise to love you for every moment of forever.
Though the sun sets and finalizes another day.
Leaving me with hope.
Hope that life with you will continue to be as beautiful.
As it is now.

Dreams of You

So many nights I dream of you.

The feelings that I have for you.

Can't get rid of them.

I wonder how a perfect love went wrong?

Wondering of the days,

our love was strong.

And when I open my eyes.

Without you.

I want a new life.

Want it with you.

If you feel the same.

Don't ever let go.

Stillness and Words

Out of the stillness,

soft spoken words.

Near or far,

close together.

Everywhere I'll be with you.

I'll love you,

always and forever.

Guided by Light

I've burned my tomorrows.

And I stand inside today.

Never to be ambushed by a lie.

Or judge for falling.

My wounded heart will rise.

How I loved you?

But the light will guide me.

To a true love forever.

Charming my thoughts.

Of magic to be brought.

And I know it'll be someone.

I'm afraid to lose.

Don't Waste Time

You really must be very stingy
with your time.
Don't waste it on people
that aren't like minded.
Don't waste it doing things
that you know aren't part of your dream plan.
Don't waste time being bitter.
Which I know I've been argumentative about.
I understand the meaning of hate.
Because in the end,
it just wastes your assets.
Time.

Respectful Boundaries

All don't deserve all places

in my life.

If you want to be in any place,

you must earn it.

If you can't earn it,

then respect it when I offer you that place.

A Picture Worth More

It's said that a picture is worth a thousand words,
but when I saw yours,
it was more than words could explain.
Your charming beauty within your pictures
are irresistible.

Wishing for Opportunities

I could wish you prosperity,

but I wish you opportunities.

I could wish you joy,

but I wish you courage.

I could wish you happiness,

but I wish you wisdom.

..... to spot the opportunity and have the courage to follow through and may that be the source of your prosperity, happiness and joy.

The Absence of Presence

I've never seen you in person,
yet I miss you.
Never felt you,
but I miss your touch.
Never kissed your soft lips,
but I long for your kiss,
that'll take my breath away.

Finding What Was Always There

Isn't too hard to see.

I was alone.

I found love where it wasn't supposed to be.

Right in front of me.

My whole universe is you.

And without you, wherever I go,

I'm half.

Nothing can change what you mean to me.

The Message in Your Eyes

I never believed in things that I couldn't see.

Until I saw the message in your eyes.

You took my heart......

My heart that lost its beat will now resume.

You make it seem like I'm close to my dream.

And I know that there will come a time.

I feel the feelings you have inside.

With my heart in your hands.

I'm hopeless because no one can take it from you.

As we build this dream together.

Standing strong forever.

A Light in the Darkness

Her soul is stained with yesterday's dust.
Her heart is stitched together with good intentions.
She has had her fair share of heartaches.
Too many have misused her trust.
Still, she shines from inside out.
Tearing the stars from her own soul,
on a clear night.
Hanging them in the sky,
to guide me home.

Oath of Loyalty

When the sun shines,
we shine together.
Told you I'll be here,
forever.
I'll always be your friend.
Took an oath that I'm sticking out,
until the end.

Rekindled Longing

Wandering shadows caressed by the night wind.

Sows its seed of longing.

Sacrificing the dream to love.

Tonight, I'm calm.

Tonight, I'm not scared.

I will meet you with hunger.

Everything I forgot,

I will find it again.

With you.

Finding Home in Your Love

I reach out for your love.

A love so strong.

Which comes from your heart.

Not just from thoughts.

I'll be with you.

Not as a love seeker.

But as a love finder and keeper.

As I finally find home in you.

We are born choosers

Neither are we born winners,

nor are we born losers.

We are born choosers.

We can all choose.

Destiny in Your Eyes

Every day I wake up.
I thank God, you're still a part of me.
Inside your eyes.
I see my destiny.
I've felt you breathe your love, so deep inside of me.
If the moon and stars fell.
They'd be easy to replace.
Because I'd lift you up to heaven.
And you'd take their place.

My Reason for Being

If I had to explain the reason,
why I find you so pretty and sweet.
I'd explain it by saying......
That you're my heart's beat.
If I had to describe you in a few words,
I wouldn't say sexy or amazing.
I'd describe you with the phrase....
You're my reason for being.

Fading Promises: Searching for Real Love

I lie awake in the morning light.

With only your promises.

Nothing left of what we had.

Time won't forget what you meant to me.

Real love wants somebody to show me?

The loneliness just fades away.

Real love isn't true anymore?

Forever Reaching for the Stars

We'll find a way to reach the stars.
In life and in love forever,
we'll always be.
Open your heart and chances are...
What you're feeling,
I'm feeling too.
With every single beat of my heart.
You're my everything.
You're the one,
the one I need.
I know it's true.
Because you're the only one for me.
I'm the only one for you.

Set Free by Love: Finding the Right Path

I've never known what was right for me.

Until that day,

when she opened my heart.

And set it free.

Every move she makes.

Hold my eyes.

I've been in love.

And alone.

That little piece inside of me,

I never thought I could.

Take control of everything.

Even though she's not real,

It's alright.

Because no one makes me feel,

the way she does.

Separated by Distance, Connected by Love

Lying in my bed as I think of you.

I wonder if you're okay.

You've touched my heart in places.

That I never even knew.

I can't believe it's you.

Can't believe it's true.

Separated by distance.

Let me take you in my arms.

Where it's easy for me to take you to the stars.

And heaven is that moment,

I look into your eyes.

More Than a Friend: My Unspoken Love

She's not my girlfriend.

But whose company I always like.

No matter how far apart we might be,

I know my thoughts include her.

She's my every smile.

I don't know,

it's just friendship,

or something more?

Whatever it is,

I just want to give her my best.

She's always welcomed in my heart's door.

I love her.

The Light Within

Ever since you were a little girl growing up....

You were fascinated by the light.

Always seeking out the light.

Yet, it wasn't until you grew up.

That you realized that the light you were always searching for.

Was hidden within you.

Do You Dare to Love Again?

Do you dare look them in the eyes?
Even if you're hurting.
While holding onto a feeling.
Looking to find love to believe in.
I'll give you my best,
I'll give my all.
I'll never leave you.
Let me feel your love.
And forget the world for a while.
Because I need you.
And that feeling you give to me.
I'll be yours,
I'll be yours again.
Just let me feel your love.

Echoes of Love Under Moonlit Skies

Listen to your heart.

Every dream.

The emptiness of breath echoes.

Yet I hear you.

By looking into your moonlit filled eyes.

Which the glow of stars follows up...

I never forget that sky,

which I sent you love.

Looking for a way when dawn stops the darkness.

To give you a hand full of warmth.

And not leave you alone.

Probably Me

You're not the easiest person,

I ever got to know.

It's hard for us both,

to let our feeling's show.

If the night turned cold.

And the stars looked down.

Know that I'm watching for you.

Because if there's one guy.

Who'd lay down his life for you and die.

Though it's hard to say.

But it's probably me.

A Prayer for Love and Healing

I pray for you to find a love,
that ignites a passion for life in your soul.
That takes all the broken parts of you,
and mends them whole.
I pray your ears fall deaf to the voices,
that once led you astray.
That you never take for granted,
the gift that is one more day.
I pray that all old afflictions are dead to you.
And can bring no joy to your heart.
I pray you find your soulmate,
of whom you never part.

Shimmering Love: From Friendship to Romance

Shimmering love.

You came along and broke my hopelessness.

You came and saved me.

Love has since blossomed within our friendship.

Take me where we can be alone.

Let me hold you in my arms.

As you softly whisper.

But it's just a dream,

I think about it.

Maybe I'm in love.

Because your memory is in my soul.

Midnight Magic: A Secret Sanctuary of Love

Paint us on a midnight canvas.

With you catching me like a falling star.

Or us meeting under the stars dancing.

Where nothing comes between us to unsettle.

And it becomes our secret sanctuary of love.

Where it's only us and the moon above.

With magic in the air between us.

And nobody hears the whispers of our hearts.

Resting on Light

No matter how tormented you might feel inside.

When you put your head on my chest.

It'll all turn to light.

Could you lie listening to my heart all day?

As I pray that you'll never leave me alone.

What would I do without you, in my life?

As I comfort you with whatever sorrow you have.

Thinking I will not heal the wounds that you have.

But no matter how tormented you might feel inside.

Just put your head on my chest.

It'll all turn to light.

All-Consuming Love

All I can think about is you.

Just to be with you,

I'd give up everything.

I don't know how to explain it.

I know the words hardly do.

They aren't even enough for me to prove to you.

You know I've always loved you.

And I always will.

For you to know the fullness of my love.

Because love is the only thing true.

Forever in Your Eyes

When I look into your eyes.

I see how much I love you.

I see forever,

in your eyes.

All I ever wanted.

Let's make a promise.

That we'll always be together.

And our love will never die.

Heart to heart.

At times it's so confusing.

But wishes can come true.

Love is right before my eyes.

When I see my world.

Faithful and true,

devoted to you.

I see only you.

The Dual Nature of Love: Gain and Loss

Love is a gain in many ways.

But it is a severe loss in a lot of ways.

Feelings and emotions take their toll.

Causing crippling pain.

Living without one soul.

Can crumble the heart.

Loving someone takes time.

Some days the sun comes out.

And the clouds clear.

That's when you see the true connection.

True love comes alive.

Full of one true connection.

Forever Your Smile

I'm your guardian angel.
I dwell inside your world.
I love you.
And it's forever.
I may be your sunlight,
or moonlight.
When the nights are cold.
I'm your sheet,
to keep you warm.
And slip into your dreams.
Or just the wind that whispers,
goodnight.
But forever I am your smile.

Until the End of Time

There's one thing that turns that gray sky blue.
When your world is full of strange arrangements.
And you know you're missing out on something.
Yet that something depends on you.
But don't let your dreams fall apart at the seams.
It takes a lot to love you.
You know it's true.
As you see through the tears.
That I'd wait a million years.
To love you until the end of time.

The Reason I Keep Going

There are days I feel hopeless.

Night's I've lost sleep.

Where my mind raced.

Wishing I could turn back the clock.

And fix what I've broken.

I'd climb·mountains.

Swim the ocean.

Just to be with you.

And keep you safe.

Because of you...

You're the reason,

I am still breathing.

The Light in You

I saw the light in you,

shining through.

When I first met you.

The moment moved me.

Your soul of beauty.

Though we're apart,

but not alone.

This soon shall pass.

Your love is something,

I can put my faith in it.

My love for you is more than you truly know.

Take me to the middle of your heart.

Where two people,

become one.

Let me feel it.

Know it's love.

A real love we only know.

Hold fast,

our love will last.

Because I'll never stop,

loving you.

Waiting for You with Open Eyes

There's a wound,
that's always bleeding.
There's a road,
I'm always walking.
Gone through days without talking.
There's comfort in silence.
So used to losing all ambition.
And struggling to maintain what's left.
There's no way around it.
But hopefully,
We'll meet again someday.
I held you then.
How bad I want to hold you now.
And I'll show you,
how to fall in love.

I'll keep waiting,

waiting for you.

Just don't close your eyes.

Forever in Love

When you came into my life.

I knew you were the one,

I've been waiting for it.

Your love found its way into my heart.

You make me dream.

It's written in your heart.

You and I were just made,

to love each other now.

You and I just have a dream.

Just forever.

Forever in love.

Forever and a day.

Journey into Your World

I came into your world.

Explored it.

Talk to your soul.

Felt your pain.

Touched your heart.

Felt your passions.

Dove into your deepest depths.

To only feel your warmth.

And know that you are real.

Hold On, I'll Find My Way Home

I know it's hard being lonely.

But remember,

I'm lonely too.

It doesn't mean,

I'll be gone forever.

Just feel in your heart,

that we won't be apart much longer.

Know in your mind,

I'll find my way back,

into your arms.

Just don't give up on me.

Don't lose hope.

Be my light,

something I rely on.

Until I find my way home.

Hopelessly Devoted to You

When you're missing me.

Look at the stars above you.

Now I'll be wishing on the same ones.

Even though I'm far away.

You never have to wonder,

where I am.

Because I'm always by your side.

Watching in slow motion.

As you keep waiting,

still anticipating love.

Whenever you reach for me,

I'll do all that I can.

Standing strong forever.

Praying I'll be the vision of your happiness.

Because I never want this feeling to end.

Now that I'm hopelessly devoted to you.

Invisible Love

Other's have promised you heaven,

to only put you through hell.

You've walked the loneliest miles.

Smiled without any style.

Kissed altogether wrong,

no intention.

But if I had told you before.

When we shared a moment that'll last,

until the end.

Perhaps you wouldn't be the same.

Am I invisible?

Because I'm in love with someone who doesn't know,

I exist.

Should I let it go?

Would you ever know?

And it's you,

Yes, it's true.

You don't even know it.

From Incomplete to Complete: Finding Happiness in Love

I wasn't happy, until you became my Queen.

My missing piece,

Now I'm complete.

From the day you came,

you gave me a whole new point of view.

If it's up to fate,

then you're my destiny.

You're a piece of my mind,

everything I've tried to find.

I've been touched by an angel.

It's impossible,

but true.

I want to spend the best days,

of my life with you.

I want your love.

And when there's talk of getting older.

You don't have to do this alone.

I hope you realize,

you'll always be beautiful in my eyes.

You and I,

will be forever young.

We want say goodbye,

because true love never dies.

Unexpected Love: Finding What I Never Knew I Needed

You're what I never saw coming.

I wanted to make you mine.

Now that I found what I never went looking for.

Gave you my heart,

not just a part.

I wrote you the most beautiful lines.

From my heart which is true.

No lying.

You're all I ever wanted.

You're the scars on my skin.

The past, I don't want to erase.

The words on my lips that have been said,

that I can still taste.

I can't sleep at night.

Realizing, you've been denying me.

When asked, if you love me?

Now there's an empty space beside me.

Which I'll keep it that way,

until you're home.

Just let me know,

Am I in your head?

Half as often as you're on my mind?

Unexpected Love: Finding What I Never Knew I Needed

You give me all my dreams.

We experienced pleasure unparalleled,

into an ocean of love,

we both fell.

I can't imagine you not by my side.

You stood by me through tough times.

So glad you're mine.

Undying passion unites our souls,

to the point of no control.

Through it all we can manage to make it,

through tough times.

I keep my dreams alive until the right time.

Clinging to what I know and letting go.

I want to love you,

give all my love to you.

I'll never do anything to hurt you.

With love we'll always make it.

Said I'll never let you,

I'd never let you fall.

Because if you didn't have this chance,

then never did I.

Meant to Be: A Journey to You

Close your eyes.

And see that we're meant to be.

I'll come after you,

we'll make it through.

I don't know where.

But I'm heading out to be with you.

I'll find you there.

And the risk is what we'll find.

My love will last forever.

In my heart,

you're number one.

All I need.

Forgive me for feeling this way.

But I miss my best friend,

my better half.

Never let go.

For the passing years will show,

that you'll always grow,

evermore beautiful in my eyes.

Changing for Our Future: My Heart Belongs to You

I don't care what we've both been through.

I'll try to change my ways for you.

Be a better man.

Change my past if I could.

But let's think about our future.

So, I can make you dream again.

I give you,

my heart.

For all that it's worth.

Everything in this world is for you.

You can ask me anything.

Don't be afraid.

I'll tell you like it is.

This feeling is so real.

You're my heart.

My everything.

Until the end of time,

my heart belongs to you.

Can't you see in my eyes,

I love you.

You'll never have to question my heart,

I love you.

My loves for you,

I love you.

Learning to Love: The Journey of Pain and Change

I wished someone would have told me.

That if I wanted love,

I'd have to go through pain.

If I wanted love,

I'm going to have to learn to change.

If I wanted trust,

I was going to have to give some.

The older I got, the voices in my head,

made me think twice.

But my flaws and scars are yours.

Your heart has a story with mine.

Though it took us a while.

Through our share of mistakes.

Yet no one can lift me,

catch me the way that you do.

I want you in my arms.

How long will I hold you?

As long as you want me to.

Because as long as the stars are above you.

Is how long,

I'll love you.

Tears of an Angel's Cry

Rain falling,

from the sky.

Tears of an angel's cry.

Heart's floating.

On the breeze.

And the only thing,

I want to feel better tonight...

Do you love me?

Discovering Love in the Unseen Parts of Me

You found parts of me,

I didn't know it existed.

And in you I found love.

I no longer believed it was real...

Guided by Your Light

I was lost within the darkness.

I said I'd never fall.

Even when I'm not who I want to be.

Ups and downs.

The days of doubt.

When I felt I've lost my way?

You stayed right beside me.

What would I be without you?

You're the sun in my sky.

Life without you is a lie.

You're my strength and power.

Together is how we must be.

We mean you and me.

I want you in my arms.

How long will I hold you?

As long as you want me to.

As long as the stars are above you.

Is how long I'll love you.

Watching You Soar: My Love from Another Shore

I'm here, just on another shore.

Sometimes I sit and wonder,

How are you feeling?

Always in your corner watching you soar.

I can't convince you that I love you for a living.

I'll open my heart.

And show you inside.

If you'll open your eyes.

And see who I am.

And not who you want me to be.

I'm up for anything that makes you smile.

Want my affection, that's my intention.

We all make mistakes.

I'm telling you exactly what it is.

Not because I know,

That's what you want to hear.

So, if you have a dream,

chase it.

Because a dream want chase you back.

Homecoming

Looking out on a summer's day.

Swirling clouds of violet haze.

I hope you know you're home to me.

It's like you never knew your worth.

When all hope was lost inside.

They couldn't love you.

Still your love was true.

I've been searching for you.

Waiting for you.

I understand what you tried to say to me.

I could have told you.

This world was never meant for one,

as beautiful as you.

As my wounds mend.

I only suffer the fall for love.

Eternally Yours

I told myself that you are the one.

I want you to know,

you'll be the one.

That I'll love the most.

Be the one I need.

I won't give up.

Because I know so much,

can come from nothing.

You were my fantasy.

You're more than a friend.

You're now my reality.

And I can't imagine my life without you.

Because I love you,

through eternity.

Through all of time.

Together, We Soar: A Love That Lasts Forever

When we come together,

we're the best of who we are.

Take my hand.

We don't need wings to fly.

In your eyes reflects a time for us.

Your smile lights up my life.

With the moments we collect.

Through failures, tears we kept.

With every fearful step.

I find in your touch, there's tenderness.

That soothes all pain.

The future lies between us both.

I'll be your soldier.

Fighting for your dreams.

Because you're my destiny.

I know you can't see.

All the things you mean to me.

If we work together.

I know it could be serious.

This can last forever.

Because I never knew a love like this before.

Beyond Good: Flying High to Succeed

There's no other way for me.

That's the way it must be.

Yet I wonder...

Should I try?

Am I strong enough?

Because being good won't be good enough.

I must try,

got to fly.

Even if I fail.

That's the way it must be.

Because to me being good isn't good enough.

It'll never be good enough.

So, when I fly,

I'll fly high enough.

I'll need special wings,

so far to go.

From so far below.

The Strength in Rejection: Reflections on Masculinity and Happiness

I'm grateful to you.

Rejection makes a man stronger.

I believe that you can't call yourself a real man.

Unless you can laugh off all the bad stuff that happens to you.

Or at least used as writing material.

So, a man's only job is to be strong.

Kind of...

But that isn't the entire story.

Basically, the pursuit of happiness isn't for us.

Stop trying to act, so call if there weren't,

any woman around.

There would be no rejection either.

Waiting to Learn Our Truth

She's scared of love.

Because she's emotionally damaged.

She holds everything in.

I see her.

When no one else did.

Yet I wait.

Hoping to learn our truth.

Before it's too late.

I hold her while we wait.

Moonlit Love

As I look at you tonight.

Soft moonlight on your face.

How you shine.

Just to look into your eyes.

Takes my breath away.

It was no accident,

me finding you.

When I hold you in my arms?

I hold everything.

There are no words.

To show my gratitude.

I've got all I'll ever need.

When our two hearts joined.

Empty Space Beside Me

I can't sleep at night.

Realizing, you've been denying me.

When asked,

if you love me?

Now there's an empty space beside me.

Which I'll keep it that way,

until you're home.

Just let me know,

Am I in your head?

Half as often as you're on my mind?

More Than Just a Memory

It's going to take time.

A little time to think things over.

I can't stay,

Yes, I know.

Love was sweet.

But our worlds can never meet.

So, I'll cry just a little...

because I love you so.

Within the night's,

I still hear your voice.

Now that love is gone.

But I can't find the words.

When the sun goes down.

The part of me that's you,

will never die.

I'll always remember us.

Because you're more than just a memory.

Unexpected Love: When You're What I Never Saw Coming

You're what I never saw coming.

Yet wanted to make you mine.

Now that I've found,

what I never went looking for.

Gave you my heart,

not just a part.

I wrote you the most beautiful lines.

From my heart, which is true.

No lying.

You're all I ever wanted.

You're the scars on my skin.

The past, I don't want to erase.

The words on my lips that have been said.

That I can still taste.

Only Half of Me

Every night I lie awake.

I slide my hand across the sheets.

Pretend you're there.

Because I want the night...

For me and you.

But I remind myself that the bed,

is only half of me.

As I close my eyes tight.

And make love to you all night.

Love's Precious Gift

You're the precious one that could have only come from above.

Let me take care of your broken heart,

and show you how to fly.

Let me hold you gently by the hand,

and kiss your tears goodbye.

Let me lead you to tomorrow's light,

and out of the needless rain.

Let me do all these to let you see,

our fates are intertwined.

I close my eyes and see perfection,

in your smile.

It presents a love,

not felt in a long while.

No one before has possessed my heart,

such as you.

You're the precious gem,

I've waited to find.

As I carry you silently in my soul.

I wonder if the more that I know you.

The more I must ask,

could this be love?

Crossing the Line to You

I've waited all my life,
to cross this line.
To the only thing that's true.
And that's to find a best friend,
I can sleep with them.
Make love to.
Dream and live with.
A life partner that I can build with.
That I can trust,
with my heart.
Somebody I'm not afraid to lose,
because I know they'll always be there.
A relationship with love and loyalty.
It's time to try anything to be with you.
I know when I go.
I'll be on my way to you.

Waiting at Heaven's Gates

Lord, when I die.

I want to live on the outskirts of heaven.

Even in King James.

It says there's a mansion,

just for me.

But I promised someone,

I'd wait at heaven's gates.

I love her and made a promise,

"I'll wait for you"

I know it's a sin to tell someone something,

and not keep your word.

I don't care how long it takes.

Tell Saint Peter, I can't come in.

Without my best friend and love.

All There Is to Me

I follow my heart,
It leads me to her.
I know she has mountains to climb.
Her beautiful smile gives me a crystal-clear picture,
of what heaven looks like.
Hearing her voice in my mind.
Leaves me all day long,
holding on.
To moments,
these feelings.
Because she's all there is to me.

Love Beyond Distance

When I think of you.

Far across the distance.

And spaces between us.

I see you; I feel your touch.

You're here in my heart.

Near, far, wherever you are.

I'm always by your side.

Though sometimes it's hard to find the words.

To tell you how much you mean to me.

Your love touched me one time.

The moment lasts forever.

Love lives in our hearts, always will.

And if I did anything right in my life.

It was when I gave my heart to you.

Love is a Decision

Love is a decision,

not a feeling.

To love is to want the good of the other.

It's nothing about feelings.

Love is a positive decision,

of whom we are as people.

You must decide to love.

To like someone is a sentimental thing.

But to love someone is a positive decision.

It's hard.

It takes work.

It's a measure of who you are,

as a person.

It's your decision to love.

In a world so full of hate.

Forever and Always

\Words aren't enough to express how special you are to me.

If I had to tell you a hundred times,

of how much "I love you"

I will never go weary.

How can I let go of someone who brought so much joy in my life?

Never.... never will I let go.

I'll love you always and forever.

Forever.... I'll stay by your side.

Forever.... I'll be your companion.

Forever.... I'll do anything for you.

Forever.... I'll bring you sunshine.

Forever.... I'll comfort your tears.

Forever.... My love will be true.

Forever.... I'll love only you.

A Message to My Troubled Brother

I know you've experienced a lot.

Try turning your anger into peace.

You've made me proud.

You're the greatest.

Even though your name is in the streets.

With every new day,

I try to maintain it.

Just remember that your brother and I have been there.

In your corner since the day you were born.

Know that we love you.

Silent Communication

It's hard to find someone.

Whom I can communicate,

even in complete silence.

But I find that someone,

in you.

Stay

Before I say another word,

let me tell you "I love you."

Let me hold you close.

Because there's an empty place inside me.

That only you can fill.

There's been times you must've thought,

I failed you.

Not because of someone else.

Because you were the first love.

I've ever had before.

All the things,

I've ever said.

I swear it is still true.

For no one else can have the part of me,

I gave it to you.

I couldn't blame you if you turned and walked away.

But with everything I feel inside.

I'm asking you,

to stay.

You Colored My Heart Red

You came into my empty heart.

In ways,

I can't say no.

You broke down walls.

For your love,

to pass through.

I never resisted you,

in doing so.

You colored my heart red.

I never feared you.

You feel my warmth.

Let it be known.

A home of love in you,

I need it.

The warmth from within,

isn't lust alone.

But a fire of my undying affection.

Burning with hope,

and faith.

But one true love,

that my heart always keeps.

The Harsh Reality of Life

Wake up to reality....
Nothing ever goes as planned,
in this accrued world.
The longer you live,
the more you'll realize.
That the only things that truly exist,
in this reality are merely pain, suffering and futility.
Listen....
Everywhere you look in this world,
wherever there's light,
there will always be shadows to be found as well.
If there's a concept of victors,
the vanquished will also be.
The selfish intent wanting to preserve peace,
initiates wars.

In hatred is born in order to protect love.

There are nexuses.

Casual relationships,

that can't be separated.

Forever Grateful

I'll never forget the day,

We started talking.

Because that day,

I met my best friend.

Somebody that I want to have,

in my life forever.

And I'll forever be grateful,

for that day.

Because I met you.

For all this searching you're the best thing,

that I've found.

I don't always find the words,

to say.

But I think about you,

constantly.

Whether it's on my mind,

or in my heart.

And it assures me,

that I'm never alone.

Lost in the Sea of Regret

Here I am drowning in the sea of misery.
The trust you put under my arms is questioning,
my dignity after losing you.
Have I failed in parenting?
I wasn't away for any vacation,
nor was I hanging with friends.
I went to work, to make a living to pay bills.
The moment I took my eyes off you.
Wings of an eagle snatched you away,
from me.
All I've lost on the crashing waves.
I thought I was standing,
but sinking.
My strength is almost gone.
How can I carry on?

Chains of yesterday surround me.

Tell me how far is north from south?

I'll come by giving myself away.

As the unheard tears of yours,

keeps me awake tonight.

And forever.

Unconditional Love

I see it in your eyes.

You feel my heart,

my love.

You've found my love true.

It's unconditional love.

You knew it from the start.

When I tell you, I love you.

I don't say it out of habit,

to make conversation.

I say it to remind you.

You're the best thing that ever happened to me.

Let's stay the way we are right now.

Looking into the future.

As far as we can see.

That a lifetime will allow.

Let’s make each tomorrow,

the best it can be.

My Heart and Soul Await You

My mind desires for a fresh start for you.

I have given you my heart.

My soul.

I wait for you.

Search for you.

Dream of you.

Now it's up to you.

To take me to the moon or heaven.

The stars decorate the sky for you.

Take me to your galaxy.

I'll accept everything.

Whatever you will offer.

I shall never disagree.

The spring displays color for you.

The rain drops desire for you.

And my blood flows in my heart for you.

Empath

You have a soft heart,

a pure soul.

Everyone has gone through something,

that has changed them in a way,

that they could never go back,

to the person they once were.

That's why you feel everything so deeply.

Forever in Your Heart

I searched deep within my soul.
Within my fears and doubts.
And all that I've found true.
To know my feelings for you are forever.
Keep me in your heart for a while.
Even when you're doing simple things around the house.
Think of me and smile.
Hold me in your thoughts.
Take me to your dreams.
Keep the fires lit.
I'll be right next to you.
Touch me as I fall into view.
And keep me in your heart for a while.

Embracing the Better Me

I'm a huge fan,

of who I'm becoming.

He's good.

He's happy.

He's trying,

to do great things.

I like him.

Forever in Your Heart

We knew that the day we started.
We were meant to be.
If only I would let you.
I had so much joy whenever you,
were part of my life.
I still dream about you.
But it's only been dark,
since you're gone.
Now that I'm living without you.
I know that you're broken hearted.
And you've cried so many tears.
Left alone to face your fears.
Now that we've let love slip away.
And having problems,
we can solve them in time.
If I could work this life out my way.

I would spend it being close to you.

But you're so far away.

What I'm trying to say is that,

I miss and still love you.

I need you in my life.

Because I still believe we have a chance.

It seems believing,

is worth the wait.

Everything stops for a moment,

becomes an echo in the rain.

I see love,

in your naked face.

The warm breath,

of certainty.

Flames of color.

No woman has loved me,

as you do.

Through My Eyes

If only you could see,
through my eyes.
Then you'd know,
that been with you.
Is an endless adventure.
The journey we're traveling on,
to each town, city or state.
Wouldn't look the same,
if you weren't by my side.
To experience all of the wonders of this world.
There's no greater beauty,
then sharing each moment with you.

Living for Others

It's not mine to take.
Do I stand tall or fall?
People say that I care.
But nothing do I give.
They say I have purpose.
Yet, just want me to live.
Oh, how I've lived for others.
Have I lived because I'm weak?
Or lived to only die inside?
I sit and I welcome.
Waiting for the day,
I give into defeat
As within my mind I think,
I truly did belong.
As I decay.

Our Love Unfolds

Make me wish.

Make me dream.

A steamy passion.

Wants to scream.

Just make me touch.

Your precious folds.

Even in silence.

Our love unfolds.

Sweet Ecstasy

Come let me taste your lips.
Let me find them sweet.
As our bodies get wrapped up in pleasure.
Entangled in the sheets.
One touch of your body.
Will leave me trembling with desire.
When you gaze into my eyes.
My heart beats faster.
With the thought of you.
Craving to be your slave.
Thriving to please my master.
Come let me taste your body.
Let me find its taste is sweet.
Which is sure to bring us to ecstasy.
Making us feel we're in heat.

First and Forever: A Love Like No Other

You are my first experience,

with everything.

Love, intimacy and heartbreak.

No other woman has ever measured up,

to what you give me.

Or how you make me feel.

Growing Stronger Through Change

I know that times are changing.

For something new.

That means you too.

What started out as friendship.

Has grown stronger.

Even though you've been through hell.

Holding the ashes to prove it.

You have scars.

I subdued my fears.

Never wanting to cause you any sorrow.

Or pain.

Instead see you smiling.

Because you're not meant to be broken forever.

Growing Stronger Through Change

You've brought me back to life.

Set my heart on fire.

You're my light.

I need you to warm these lonely nights.

Your body is like the holy grail.

I've got to find it.

As you love me like you do.

And find trust in when I say,

I love you.

Forever My Always

You give me hope and bring me joy.

You're proof all I need is you.

Looking into your eyes.

I'll give you my love with sweet surrender.

Because you'll forever be my always.

Broken Love, Unfulfilled Dreams

When I saw you.

I felt a great need for you.

In your eyes you were hiding the pain.

I felt it without words.

I built up feelings.

Though some will want to own you.

Use you.

And abuse you.

Leaving your happiness.

Into sadness.

Because cheating love brings more suffering.

Knowing that pain is better,

than picking up sadness.

All because love has been broken.

This is why love is just a dream.

Unfulfilled dreams.

She's lonely and distant from warm hands.

No matter how much we love each other.

She lived on memories.

If you ever chose to fly.

Fly with choices.

Not with wings that didn't try.

Our love isn't broken within all of this.

Because here we are.

Another long day waiting.

But this is how our life is going.

Patience is a virtue.

So I'll never be fed up.

Waiting for you.

Secluded Pleasures: A Journey of Passion and Love

Let me take you away.

To a secluded place and lie you down.

As I make you forget who I am.

Where I come from.

Let the only name you whisper be mine.

I'll kiss you.

As your toes curl as my hands glide along your curves.

Whispering to you in your ear.

As your moans are lifted in the breeze.

With my mouth remembering your body.

Making you shiver as I spread you.

My tongue enticing, seducing, forcing you to lose control.

Watching as your body writles for me.

Arching, lifting and rolling in pleasure.

Licking and sucking as you beg for me.

Letting you see the stars.

I'll crawl over you, cuddling you in my arms.

As we look into each other's eyes.

Sink deeply into you, taking your breath as I fill you.

Allowing you to feel every ridge, vein throb in you.

As your mouth opens in pleasure as you align your body with mine.

Telling me I belong to you.

As I take you away.

Come closer.

Until I no longer know where I end.

And you begin.

Put your arms around me.

I want to hold you forever.

In this life your love is only what matters to me.

Love which fills my life, makes my heart beat.

When I am listening, your soft love whispers.

Your touch warms my heart.

There is nothing more beautiful than surrendering to you.

Embracing Love

Lean on my heart.

For me to forget where my end is.

For you to forget when you begin.

Make me feel your hands around me.

I can't imagine my life without you.

Love is All that Matters

In this life your love is only what matters to me.
Love which fills my life, makes my heart beat.
When I am listening to your soft lips whisper.
Your touch warms my heart.
There is nothing beautiful as surrendering to you.

Past Life Connection

Feels like I knew you in a past life.

You and I seem so natural.

How I feel with you.

It feels good to just be real.

All I ever wanted.

All I ever looked for.

Is the comfort of feeling safe,

with you.

Under the Milky Way Tonight

Your love makes me alive.

You make my heart burn with,

Love fire lasting to the end of time.

I can see in your eyes, us, our love.

You are my flower, my love forever........

You are the star on the mountain.

Shining through the black rivers of the night.

All my burning, longing goes to you.

Meet me on the Milky Way.

And I will from deep wells scoop kisses and love.

Until we both drown with passion.

When this place gets kind of empty.

And our breath fades with the light.

I think of a loveless fascination.

Which I see in your sparkling eyes.

And I find it quite peculiar.

It led you here, despite your destination.

Under the Milky Way tonight.

Inside My Soul

Inside my soul.

Pounds a burning, longing

Show me the shape of lust.

Scratch red words on my white skin.

Nothing.....

Less than nothing.

Can stop us now.

I want the night.

For just you and me.

I want to tease you.

Please you.

Show you that I need you.

I want your body.

I want to do it right.

I promise to give it to you.

Just the way you like.

Waiting for our Truth

Afraid to love.

Because she's emotionally damaged.

She holds everything in.

I saw her.

When no one else did.

How I make her smile.

Yet I wait.

Hoping to learn our truth.

Holding her while we wait.

Halo of Love

I see a halo above you.
Your eyes shine like the stars in the sky.
Planets align when I touch you.
I just want to be the reason why.
Why you smile all the time?
Be the only one you need.
You know that I love you.
You're the one that's in my dreams.
At night when I go to sleep.

A Warm Sun in a Field of Dreams

At rising dawn.

You're like the warm sun.

In a pasture of sprouted flowers.

Where a million dreams.

Opens like a fantasy.

You're full of love.

For me in your heart.

Where wishes are caressed.

Leaving love and memories.

With your hands.

Giving me moments that warms my heart.

As I love you passionately.

And sleep comes within the night.

Love Across Time and Space

I have loved you since the beginning.

Happiness with you is so desired.

I drifted into your mind.

You became my soul.

As the moon worships the sun.

Guided by love that has no beginning,

or end.

Not seeing one another.

Words linked our worlds together.

I sent you my heart and love through lightning.

So you wouldn't forget me as the days go by.

Someday your heart will spark light for me.

And I'll let you taste my love in reality.

Anchor of Love

In a sea of heartache.

It's pulling you under.

Put your arms around me.

Let go of that old memory.

I'll be here holding you.

When your heart is a mess.

Know that I love you.

In my heart you remain.

Everytime I close my eyes,

I see you.

And how you I want to live my life,

with you.

You're the only one I'll ever love.

So long as the sun is shining.

The oceans are blue.

I still love you.

The People We Meet

Fate isn't stupid.

It brings you people,

either those you want or those who need you.

At any stage of life.

And no matter how strange life's twists and turns may seem.

Sometimes even unbelievable......

Know that these are the people you need right now......

or you save them.....

or they save you.

Among the many faces that cross your life,

you'll meet a person who'll completely change your life.

You can meet them now, tomorrow, in a year, in 5, 10 years.

But you'll definitely be together,

no matter what.

Your heart will feel it right away,

even if your logic tells you again that you're wrong.

And when your hearts begin to beat together at the same rate,

no matter how different time zones, or distance between continents you'll understand.

Love is joy, admiration, comfort and warmth.

Next to the person,

you love.

Accepting All of Me

I'll give you all of me.
Heart, scars and all of the above.
Just tell me you would accept me?
Tell me that you see,
want and desire me.
I want you to whisper my name,
as I hold you tightly.
I want to share your secrets,
dreams and aspirations.
As we connect our bodies intertwine in ways,
people only see in erotic movies.
Eyes closed, lip biting, hands clawing.
Feel me as I'm longer on the outside,
but inside.
Feel our tongues dance to the sweetest rhymes.

Feel that our dreams and fantasies are no longer,

dreams and fantasies.

It has become our reality.

Love in a Photograph

You left a mark in my mind,
that can't be erased.
Took a piece of my heart,
that can't be replaced.
I don't care about the two of us from different worlds.
Heaven can wait,
we're only watching the skies.
I give what I got,
to stand like a rock.
Beside you.
I lost my love to you.
And hope you know.
It's hard to grow old without a cause.
In time your eyes will lose their shine.
But I keep this love in a photograph.

When I'm alone in my dreams,

I am searching for you.

Hoping I'll find myself in your arms.

To show me that love,

looks like you.

Daydreaming

Where will my thoughts wander,

and take me today?

Will I try ,

and keep my daydreams at bay?

Or will I unlock my imagination,

and let them fly away......

The Promise of Us Together

It's in between where days and nights submerge.

That we find our minds with indecent entanglements.

Leaving us tasting the future with a promise of us together.

You still find me in your twirled world of words.

Wordless in a dazed wonder.

Of how the emotions seem so otherworldly.

Breaking down old walls, soothing heartache, loss and struggle.

Now breathless, hoping we've found a chance of love.

To bath our souls in encouragement, love......

It tenderly embraces to see us into a future of old age.

Loving each other for our flaws, thoughts of love.

Blessed to still hold a gaze that knows,

we were somehow always meant to be.

Treasure Her: A Love Letter to Self and Other

Treasure her.

Protect her peace,

and make time for her,

and when she comes to you,

aflame with passion and stars in her eyes,

and asks you to dance......

leap without a thought.

What comes from that is pure art,

in whatever way you express it.

Treasure and protect that spark in her eyes,

and always put her first,

in whatever way you can.

Your soul is your first love,

and defines all that follows.

Hopelessly Devoted to You

When you're missing me .
Look at the stars above you.
Know I'll be wishing on the same ones.
Even though I'm far away.
You never have to wonder,
where I am.
Because I'm always by your side.
Watching in slow motion.
As you keep waiting,
still anticipating love.
I'll do all that I can.
Standing strong forever.
Praying I'll be the vision of your happiness.
Because I never want this feeling to end.
Now that I'm hopelessly devoted to you.

Finding Our Way Back to God

We are all prisoners,
locked into a world of space and time.
We have control over our actions.
But our actions are actually,
our reactions.
To occurrences in time and space.
The pattern of which is sent by forces.
Beyond our very limited comprehension.
Each person in this world.
Is here to find his way back,
to God.
God manifests into our lives.
Problems that we must solve and overcome.
In order to become masters,
of our own lives.

Once we have overcome the trials and tests.

Given to us on earth.

We will then be able to become,

the company to God.

That we originally were intended to be.

God's Promise of Love

If I could, I'd write for you a rainbow.
And splash it with all the colors of God.
And hang it in the window of your being.
So that each new God's morning.
Your eyes would open first.
To hope and promise.
If I could, I'd wipe away your tears.
And hold you close forever in shalom.
But God never promised I could write a rainbow,
never promised I could suffer for you,
only promised I could love you.
That I do.

For Love's Sake

I'm willing to sacrifice.

Even though I hardly show anyone.

That I know how to fall in love.

But if that's the only way.

To make us happy.

Only you will know.

Because the woman I love.

Is you.

Home in Your Eyes

In your eyes is where I looked.
When I told you.
I loved you.
Because I wanted you to know.
What I felt.
In your eyes is where I find salvation.
From the harm of this world.
In your arms is where I find comfort.
Protected and loved.
But I always look into your eyes.
There I'm home.

More Than Words

I want to give you more than words.
I want to love you in every kind of way.
I trust in you and know that you're with me,
forever.
Whenever everything seems to fail.
I want be shaken,
or moved.
Because in darkness,
you're my light.
When I'm hopeless,
you're my guide.
Can I tell you something for what it's worth?
With you heaven,
is a place on earth.

Missing You in Silence

When silence isn't quiet.

I want you to know,

I miss you.

Like the stars miss the sun,

in the morning sky.

Though we have each other.

But there's days where I feel broken down and tired.

I can't seem to find the fighter,

within myself.

Making me wish that the sunshine goes away.

But in spite of the ache.

I continue to pray that life goes my way.

With the intention to rise unafraid.

Because all we need is hope.

And for you,

I'll move mountains.

Finding My Way Home

I've been down.
Spent my life stuck in a pattern.
I've been the upper side of down.
The inside of out.
I push through the pain,
rise from the flames.
Yet I have an open mind.
You want see me quit,
no I'm not giving in.
As I look around at a beautiful life.
And wondering why.
I don't want to gain this world.
But take my time for me.
So maybe tomorrow.
I'll find my way home.

Fixing a Broken Heart

Let me fix your broken heart.
It's an endless aching need.
Your hearts afraid of breaking.
And never takes the chance.
It's the ones that want to be taken,
we regret the most.
My heart has been borrowed,
and yours has been blue.
Secrets I've held in my heart.
Are harder to hide than I thought.
Can you feel my heart?
I'll wait for you.
There's a lot of ways to say what I want to say to you.
There's poems, promises and dreams that might come true.
But I rather whisper in your ear.

I just want to be yours.

Let you know how much it means,

just having you.

Even when your golden hair,

fades to silver.

Can we always be this close forever,

and ever?

The Great Divide

The great divide that separates you and me.
Is only a heartbeat,
not an open sea.
The separation of a body from its soul.
Is the story of you and me.
That is yet untold.
Words can not explain how much you mean to me.
Nothing could ever compare or even ever be.
You gave me a new life,
that'll never be the same.
I just want you to know,
somebody loves you.
Though your heart grew cold.
Free yourself from mistakes that build the wall in your heart.
And see love's right beside you.

The miles will fade away.

A place in time still belongs to us.

No one can ever take your place.

Always remember,

you're never too far away.

Love Beyond Words

Not seeing one another,

words linked our worlds together.

I knew in my heart.

Nothing worth having is easy.

But you're worth any struggle.

Praying I'll be the version of your happiness.

I want to give you my best.

You're always welcomed in my heart's door.

I'm not trying to fix you,

I can't heal you.

I'm just trying to show you,

how beautiful broken is.

Know that I love you.

In my heart you remain.

Every time I close my eyes,

I see you.

And how I want to live my life,
with you
You're the only one I'll ever need.
So long as the sun is shining.
The oceans are blue.
I still love you.
A love so strong which comes from the heart.
Not just thoughts,
not as a love seeker.
But as a love finder and keeper.
As I find home in you.
Life's a journey,
not just a destination.
As long as there's hope,
there's a possibility.
With you, possibility there's life.
Without love we feel nothing,
without dreams we accomplish nothing.

And nobody hears the whispers of our hearts.
Do you know why I came into this world?
So that I could absorb the riches of your love.
And give you more love in return.
That my dear is the singular purpose of my life.
Falling in love is only half of what I want.
Staying in love with you forever, is the other.
Don't ask me again,
if I ever need or love you.
My words are already laid before you.
You're everything I ever needed.
I love you more than words can define,
feelings can express,
thoughts can be imagined.
Every love story is beautiful,
but ours I like the most.

Unspoken Desires

Secrets I've held in my heart.

It Is harder than I thought

Maybe I just want to be yours.

So take this beating in my heart.

And come finish what you started..

Confession of Love

I've got something to tell you.

I believe you ought to know.

It's coming from my heart,

not my head.

But this feeling doesn't come along everyday.

I'm not trying to make you uncomfortable.

So now I got the chance to tell you.

You'll never know,

if you don't know now.

Here in my heart,

I just long for you.

I miss you.

I care about you.

If there's some other way to prove that I love you,

I don't know how.

I want to spend my life with you.

Summer's Love

Look out on a summer's day.

Swirling clouds of violet haze.

I hope you know you're home to me.

It's like you never knew your worth.

When all hope was lost inside.

They couldn't love you.

But still your love was true.

I've been searching for you.

Waiting for you.

I understand what you tried to say to me.

This world was never meant for one.

As beautiful as you.

My wounds are mending.

I only suffer the fall for love.

True Love's Promise

Looking in your eyes.

I have to tell you what I've been feeling for a while.

I'm sure these feelings aren't lies.

I'm filled with thoughts of you.

This love I'm feeling for you.

Is true love.

My heart burns with passion.

I want to spend the rest of my life with you.

Never before has someone been more.

You're my whole life.

My whole world.

You're my true love.

So much I want to give you.

Put your hand in my hand.

I'll take you to the good times.

See you through the bad times.

We can build this dream together.

Treasured Friendship

Treasured friend,

I'm so glad I found you.

Our friendship is a gift we share.

Thank you friend, for all the things,

that mean so much to me-

For cheering and supporting me.

For things I can't explain.

What I'm trying to say.....

Is with all your support you're giving.

You're giving doesn't go unnoticed.

You're such a pleasure in life.

A joy to me.

Our friendship bond was meant to be.

I think of you with great delight.

Other people may fill my day,

but never in such an important way.

I'll cherish you my whole life.

You're all of this and more.

Because you mean so much,

to me.

More than I can express.

You are my Light

I was lost within the darkness.

I said I'd never fall.

Even when I'm not who I want to be.

Ups and downs.

For the days of doubts.

When I've felt,

I've lost my way.

You stay right beside me.

What would I be without you?

You're the sun in my sky.

Life without you is a lie.

You're my strength and power.

Together is how we must be.

We meaning you and I.

I want you in my arms.

How long will I hold you?

As long as you want.

As long as the stars are above you.

Is how long,

I'll love you.

Lessons of Love

I wished someone would have told me.

That if I wanted love,

I'd have to go through the pain.

If I wanted love,

I'm going to have to learn to change.

If I wanted trust,

I was going to have to give some.

The older I get,

the voices in my head.

Made me think twice.

But my flaws and scars are yours.

Your heart has a story with mine.

Though it took us a while.

Through our share of mistakes.

Yet no one can lift me, catch me the way that you do.

I want you in my arms.

How long will I hold you?

As long as you want me to.

As long as the stars are above you.

Is how long,

I'll love you.

Love Across the Distance

Even though you're far away.

I don't care what we've both been through.

I'll try to change my ways for you.

Be a better man.

Change my past if I could.

But let's think about the future.

So I can make you dream again.

I give you my heart.

For all that it's worth.

Everything in this world is for you.

You can ask me anything.

Don't be afraid.

I'll tell you like it is.

This feeling is so real.

You're my heart.

My everything.

Until the end of time,
my heart belongs to you.
Can't you see in my eyes,
I love you.
You'll never have to question my heart,
I love you.
My love's for you.
I love you.
I'm here,
just on another shore.
Sometimes I sit and wonder how you're feeling.
Always in your corner watching you soar.
I can't convince you that I love you for a living.
I'll open my heart.
And show you inside.
If you'll open your eyes.
And see who I am.
And not what you want for me to be.

I'm up for anything that makes you smile.

Want my affection,

that's my intention.

We all make mistakes.

I'm telling you exactly what it is.

Not because I know,

that's what you want to hear.

Every night

Every night I lie awake.

I slide my hand across the sheets.

Pretend you're there.

Because I want the night,

for me and you.

But I remind myself that the bed is only half mine.

As I close my eyes tight.

And make love to you all night.

My World in a Picture

I've heard it said,

a picture is worth a thousand words.

When I look at you,

I see my world.

Before you came into my life,

I never knew what it felt like to love someone this much.

My heart was empty,

but now it's full of love.

I can't stop thinking about you.

You're the one person in the world.

I've come to love,

treasure and protect.

I'll always be there for you.

You're my angel.

I'll do anything for you just to ensure your happiness.

I'll go that extra mile.

With you,

we'll accomplish a lot.

Forever Yours

I told myself that you are the one.

I want you to know,

you'll be the one.

That I'll love the most.

Be the one I need.

I won't give up.

Because I know so much,

can come from nothing.

You were my fantasy.

You're more than a friend.

You're now my reality.

I can't imagine life without you.

I want to show you love through eternity,

through all of time.

Can You Be My Love and Friend?

Can you be my friend?

Because I need someone who can love me at my worst.

And see my worth.

Even when I'm the weakest one of all.

I think I'm falling.....

Falling in love with you.

I need your love.

To keep me from falling down.

To the ground.

Can I call you baby?

I want to be with you.

We can make it to the end.

Across the Distance, In My Dreams

There are hills and mountains between us.

An ocean apart.

All these miles separate.

Disappear when I dream of you.

I dream about you all the time.

Constantly thinking of you.

In my mind or in my heart.

Day after day.

I'm right here waiting for you.

And when the night comes,

it's only you and me.

Sparkle in Your Eyes

When I saw the sparkle in your eyes.

I knew that was a sparkle,

I wanted to see it everyday for the rest of my life.

Let the moon's glow be of our emotions.

The guide of our purpose.

I'll always care for you,

even though we're far from one another.

I miss you often.

A whole lot each day.

Even though we're not together.

The Light of Love

I still see who you are.

Even though you're just a shadow of yourself.

I still love who you are.

And I know deep in your heart.

You know the way back home.

Just let this light of love in.

Somewhere Out There

I close my eyes.

To only see you.

I think of two young lovers.

I know you're somewhere out there.

Somewhere far away.

I wish I could.

I wish I might.

Have a chance to hold you tight.

Whispering things in your ear.

You've been waiting to hear.

Red on a Rose

When I look into your soft,
beautiful eyes.
I'm reminded that what I feel for you,
will remain strong and true.
Like red on a rose.
When your lips first smiled at me.
I was captivated instantly.
The gaze in your willing eyes.
If I had to do it all over.
I'd do it all again.
If tomorrow,
I found one more chance to begin.
I'd love you,
all over again.
A once in a lifetime love.

We love like we've dreamed of.

The longer we love.

The memories just keep adding up.

The years and miles may separate you from me.

But for me your memories will never fade.

Inspired by a Smile

It was no accident that I found you.
There was a look in your eyes.
Like you were just part of a dream.
Nothing more,
so it seemed.
But I can't forget the picture of your smile.
Everytime I close my eyes,
you come alive.
Give it a little more time.
We'll be together.
You and I.
Then I could love you more.
Much stronger than before.
It seems like a dream.
Much more so it seems.

I found my inspiration,

with just one smile.

It still takes my breath away.

Looking into your eyes.

As I look at you tonight.

Long Distance Longing.

There's someone I've been missing.
I think that they could be the better half of me.
But they're in the wrong place,
trying to make it right.
But the fight for her is all I've ever known.
I spend my time,
with you in my mind.
I see you, and though I can't touch you,
I feel you.
No words can explain the way,
I'm missing you.
Truth is,
I don't want to miss you anymore.
Then I already do.
Falling in love in the cruelest way.

Falling for you and you're a thousand miles away.

Don't bury thoughts that you really want.

All your flaws and scars are mine.

I don't want to miss you like this.

I need your love,

your passion.

Your love that's everlasting.

I want you to know.

If I can't be close to you.

I'll settle for the ghost of you.

But I believe,

that one day,

I'll be next to you.

Rhythm of My Heart

I always thought,
I'd be a ramblin man.
Living in the moment,
never making plans.
Wondering when will my heart beat again?
Then you became the rhythm of my heart.
I don't think that you understand.
You make me a better man.
The best part of me,
is you.
Sometimes it's hard to find the words.
To tell you how much you mean to me.
If I did anything right in my life.
It was when I gave my heart to you.
Sometimes my eyes get jealous of my heart.

Because you always remain close to my heart.

And far from my eyes.

Though we're far apart,

you're not alone.

I'm there with you,

you're always in my heart.

Every day and night,

my mind is filled with thoughts of you.

As long as the sun continues to shine.

You can be that my heart,

will remain yours.

I'll wait for you,

I promise you.

I will.

I swear,

I couldn't love you more than I do,

right now.

Yet I know,

I will tomorrow.

My World with You

My life is much better with you,
I swear.
Finally found myself in a world,
that can't go around.
Without you.
I see the start of every night and everyday,
in your heart.
I get lost in your eyes.
In your arms,
I can be in no better place.
I hope that you'll stay by my side.
I'll tell you more about how I feel inside.
My touch will define how special you are.

Together, We Shine

When we come together,
we're the best of who we are.
Take my hand.
We don't need wings to fly.
In your eyes reflects a time for us.
Your smile,
lights up my life.
With the moments we collect.
Through failures,
tears we kept.
With every fearful step.
In your touch there's tenderness.
That soothes all pain.
The future lies between us both.
I'll be your soldier.

Fighting for your dreams.

Because you're my destiny.

If we work together.

I know it could be serious.

This can last forever.

Because I never knew love like this before.

I know you can't see.

All the things you mean to me.

More Than Words: A Love Worth Sharing

I know you've heard it all before.

But you're the love of my life.

And I believe there's a love you want to share.

He never understood what you were worth.

Never tried to make it work.

If it's love you're looking for,

I can give you a little more.

This euphoric bliss I'm experiencing.

Has me wrapped up in you.

And I wonder if over time if just-fell-in-love.

Transforms into something less charged,

but more stable and lasting?

Because my thoughts return to you often.

I finally feel safe and secure.

My life feels more exciting,

with this compassion I feel for you.

Eternal Love and Understanding

I hear your voice calling me.

I see you in my mind.

Not just as an illusion.

I see forever in your eyes.

I'll try until I die for you and I.

I've heard of a love that comes once in a lifetime.

I'm pretty sure that you're that love of mine.

You don't have to be a star.

I love you just the way you are.

Know that when we're one.

Love will be the lifeline.

Out where the world belongs.

To only you and I.

We'll always be one.

Our two hearts will beat as one.

Just give me true love and understanding.

For the rest of my days.

Memories of Love

It all came together.
Through my shattered eyes.
Say goodbye to yesterday.
I close my eyes,
look behind.
The tears will clear and I will not fear.
I can feel you near.
As the sun goes down.
Your path is your path,
that's what you say.
But I hope it doesn't end up this way.
I wish I could be there for you,
like you said you'd be there for me.
There's no room for wondering.
Even if you're a million miles away.

Lead with courage,
dream with your heart.
One day our paths will cross again.
In which,
I hope to make you smile again.
How sweet the memory lingers.
Of the love you gave to me.

Almost Paradise

The first time I saw your face.
I thought the sun rose in your eyes.
And the moon and stars were gifts you gave.
I hear your voice in my mind.
I know her face by heart.
Heaven and earth moves in my soul.
Sometimes I can't find the words to define.
The way I feel about someone so fine.
At night I dream.
That she is here.
It always looks the same,
true love always does.
Almost paradise.
Like we're knocking on heaven's door.
How could I ask for more?

When I see you smile.

Forever in Love

When you came into my life.
It took my breath away.
You gave me your smile.
You gave me your heart.
You gave me the feel,
I've been looking for.
I feel it everytime my heart beats for you.
And no one else.
I guess the time was right for us to say,
we'd take our time and live our lives together,
day by day.
We know our dreams can all come true.
Still we know that the road is long.
Because our love is strong.
I'm home again.

A thousand miles away from you.

A moment in time.

Forever in love.

Refusing to Let Go

Last night I could hear you crying.

Your soul is broken.

Inside you're hiding.

When the love around you is dying.

Your heart is jaded.

You've been to hell and back.

Refusing to let it show.

It feels as if your spirit is fading.

But I'm right beside you now.

How can I take the pain away?

You and I aren't an in between.

I'm tired of living,

like we're just a dream.

Just because I'm not with you.

Yet I refuse to fall.

Though I want us dreaming of dreams.

Dreaming of what we think is real.

Though, I refuse to let go.

I want let you fall tonight.

Breaking Down the Wall

This wall around my heart.
I Want to fall.
And know what true love and happiness feels like.
Then you came along and busted away a chunk,
of the wall surrounding my heart.
To only have fallen on it to break your bones,
against the stones on the ground.
But it's as if my heart is too dark to care.
As if my hope vanished,
long ago.
With so much rage within myself.
Locked within a cage.
Someday, I hope to face the real me.
When I face the hell within myself.
Trying to understand what's right and wrong.

Only then let’s give this another try.

Breaking Down the Wall

Can you take the time to unwind for me?

See I'm just a man.

Who put his dreams above all things.

And now come right into your arms.

I know that someone like you,

would come along.

So I could share my love with.

I've been turned down.

But I haven't been worried.

Because I knew that someone like you,

would come along.

My Best Friend and Life Partner

I want a best friend ,
I can sleep with them.
Make love to.
Dream and live with.
A life partner that I can build with.
That I can trust with my heart.
Somebody I'm not afraid to lose,
because I know they'll always be there.
A relationship with love and loyalty.

Defending My Heart's Longing

Sometimes my heart,

is in defense of pains,

pains of longing for you.

A Rose for the Beautiful Girl in Your Eyes

The voice in your beautiful eyes.

Is deeper than all roses.

But still I'd give to you,

the most beautiful girl in the world.

The one that holds my heart.

A beautiful rose.

Not just an ordinary single rose.

It's my love for you from my heart.

Reassuring you,

I'll love you until the end of time.

Everyday until then.

My heart will beat strong.

For all the love,

I have for you.

Longing for Forever

It wasn't hard for me,

to fall in love with you.

The hardest part is being away from you,

but I'm longing for the moment.

We'll be together.

How we may be apart,

but my love for you stays strong.

When I feel alone.

I close my eyes and I feel your arms wrap around me.

Your tender kisses and sweet whispers.

All I ever need is you.

But for now,

I'll wait for that sweet moment.

I want to hold you forever.

When it comes,

I'll hold your hand forever.

Candlelight Love

You're looking out the window.
Like a candle burning light.
Love is flowing in your eyes.
A flame that burns brighter everyday.
Now that I have you.
Nobody loves you like I do.
Isn't it funny how life just falls in place?
Somehow.
Each day unfolds.
Though separated by distance.
In this instance.
I kiss the air.
Letting you know that I care.
In the wind it's carried.
Until it finds your beautiful face.

Lost in Your Eyes

Why do I get so nervous,
when I look into your eyes?
You're everything I need,
but I didn't think I'd find.
You're someone who is worth the wait,
of all the years of my heart break.
This is the choice we take.
No one knows, but with you,
I feel hope again.
You seem to always catch my breath.
But I lose it again,
when I look at you.
I know I found the one,
I love.
When I look into your eyes,

I know it's real.

I want to spend my whole life trying,

to find a way to show you,

how I feel.

Without our love just being borrowed.

The Fire Within

Dear Heart,

There's a fire inside.

Glowing, warming.

You're a vase of love.

Of all things felt.

You're not just flesh and blood.

You bear pains.

When you forgive,

you heal.

When you let go,

you grow.

Yet you know that the hardest times in life,

we go through when we are leveling up,

from one version of ourselves to another.

Yet you hold yourself together.

Even when you feel crushed by the world.

And knowing those excuses only gives someone else an opportunity.

You have faith.

Dreaming of You

In my dreams.......

You're lying next to me.

With the sound of your breath on my neck,

the warmth of your lips on my cheek,

the touch of your fingers on my skin,

and the feeling of your heart beating with mine.

I wonder what I did to deserve this moment?

And as you're breathing easily.

I can only think about what it is that I can do tomorrow.

To be better for you,

than I was today.

You’re my completeness.

Everything I’ll ever need.
I find within your love.
With you.
All those years of searching,
I see you’ve been my destiny.
I’m not with you physically.
And in person.
To hold, kiss your soft lips.
Run my fingers through your hair.
Or trace the curves,
of your beautiful body.
But we’re closer than before.
And you will always and forever,
be in my heart.
Which is closer than anyone else.
I love you more than just words to you.

Steady Love

I'm just a boy with a thousand endings.
Yet she touched my heart.
My soul and spirit.
Gave me love,
steady love.
I want to be with her.
Be lovers and friends.
And when we hold hands.
She'll want everyone to know,
I'm her man.
I'll feel her pure intentions.
Two bodies.
Of where she ends and I begin.
Every night it's her,
I'm dreaming of.

As I keep it simple and do it right.

Even though

I'm just a man with a thousand endings.

Longing in Distance

This distance between us is to far a part,

and it pains me.

I can't even smile.

What should I do,

when I miss you?

What should I do,

when I want to see you?

It's just an unsatisfactory dream,

I'm left with.

If I only had wings....

Understand how I feel just a bit.

Your presence in my heart.

Grows bigger and bigger,

day after day.

We must always be together.

It's natural I wish for that.

I have so much I want to say.

I'm glad that I came to love you.

But what should I do,

when I miss you?

Simply wish to the moon and stars?

Reflections of Your Flame

I dream about fire in your heart.

I dream about your beauty.

I still feel warmth of your flame.

Flame which burned when I hold you in my arms.

I wonder about sparks and stars in your eyes.

Stars which shined from deepest well of my love.

I still remember when your heart was only one.

When it beat for both of us.

Silent days and nights of desire for you is left now.

Silent and quiet desire which fills my lonely life.

Through this silence, my tears, my heart drops.

Becoming a reflection, mirror of your beautiful face.

Love Among the Stars

I dream about you, my love, too.
I think about our love all the time.
Love which God made, but life split.
Powerful love which became a memory.
Memory of us living in different worlds.
In beautiful space and time lit with your powerful heart.
Only stars in my life left now are one in the night sky.
I can see our love shining there forever, untouched.
Even though love is lost, it is still alive.
It can be found, reborn...
Love ashes stayed in my heart too, my soul guards it.
With strength and power from the crevices of my heart.

Forever in Love: A Thousand Miles Away

A thousand miles away from you.

You came into my life.

Took my breath away.

You gave me a smile.

You gave me your heart.

You gave me the feel,

I've been looking for.

I feel it everytime my heart beats for you.

And no one else.

The time was right for us to say.

We'd take our time.

Still we know that the road is long.

And live our lives together,

day by day.

We know our dreams still can all come true.

We know that we'll be together.

Because our love is strong.

I'm here again.

A thousand miles away from you.

A moment in time.

Forever in love

A Place with You

You're like the sun.

Softly touching my body warmly.

In a gentle breeze.

Reminding me of your soft unspoken words.

Like a timeless dream.

In a place of peace.

Place of joy.

A place away from loneliness.

A place away from pain.

A place where two hearts beat as one.

Near or far.

That place is next to you.

Sinking in Silence

Have you ever felt so far away?

Where you believe,

in silence,

you're sinking.

Because of broken trust and broken hearts.

Where falling out of love is hard,

but falling for betrayal is worse.

Thinking that all I need is here.

Building faith,

on words and love.

Now empty promises we wear,

we know.

Take me back,

because I want to stay.

Save your tears for another.......

Another day.

Love's Tender Embrace

Take to your bed.

Where you say there's peace.

But dream of love instead.

Fate tell me it's right,

is this love at first sight?

There's more beauty in her than anyone.

As I take her by the hand.

And lead her where I will.

To make love with affection.

Give her love.

I'll sing her a love song.

With dedication and feeling.

Ones to make her wonder.

If she's feeling down,

feeling low.

Let her just think of me.

Remembering she's everything I need.

And that I'm secure with her.

She inspires me to try.

But if I were to fall.

Let me fall at her door.

Because she has loving arms to hold me.

Sweet Surrender

Come closer,
until I no longer know where I end,
and you begin.
Put your arms around me,
all I want to do is hold you forever.
The thought of our bodies together.
Warm, touching, moving slowly.
Kissing and whispering things.
I believe that you were sent into my life,
to give me something to fight for.
To show me there's love in this world.
To give me hope and to bring me joy.
You're proof all I need is you.
Looking into your eyes.
I'll give you my love with sweet surrender.

Because you'll forever,

be my always.

Going the Distance

A voice keeps saying this is where I'm meant to be.

I'll find my way if I can be strong.

Every mile will be worth my while.

When I go the distance.

I'll be where I belong.

To embrace my fate.

Led to you.

I want accept defeat.

I'll face the world's harm.

Until I find my welcome waiting,

in your arms.

Always with Me

You're in my heart.
Part of my soul.
When I close my eyes.
I see your face.
The curve of your smile.
The sparkle in your eyes.
Your golden hair.
I hear your voice saying my name.
I feel your touch.
As I breathe in your scent.
Your hand in mine.
Where it always fits so perfectly.
In my mind.
And when I close my eyes.
You'll always be there.

For Love's Sake

Your heart was broken.
I got you off of your knees.
Put you back on your feet.
I said, I'd catch you if you fall.
As you escaped the dreams in your mind.
Which I took and made them mine.
Afraid to leave you on your own.
Took it so far to keep you close.
I gave all I could for love.
Even if my destiny was lying.
For the one I held dear,
I held close.
Remind me of my emptiness.
In this sorrow,
so I might shed a tear.

Because I gave all I could.....

For love.

Miles Apart, Heart Together

Everyday that we spend together.
Is a day that I'll cherish forever.
Though miles away, I wait for that text.
Since a text is the most we can do.
To see how you are and how your day was.
So glad to have a friend miles away.
But that doesn't stop me from missing you.
Yet when it comes to my feelings.
My heart only beats for you.
Your smile, laugh and gentle touch.
Your pure and wonderful loving heart.
When I close my eyes,
I feel them.
Even though we're apart.
Sometimes you'll come find me.

When I'm in bed asleep.

You'll always be my friend.

Not just a simple friend,

but a special friend at that.

Friendship or Love?

You walked into my life.
Held out your arms.
And my heart and soul,
you did hold.
Never knew I meant so much.
That your heart was worth enough to care.
I started to dream of you every night.
Melted the coldness of your heart.
With the warmth of my light.
I ended up falling for you,
how could I not?
But you told me it's not the same.
For you only think of me as a friend.
I can't understand this,
the wrong messages you did send.

That touched me as a lover.

Here I am in love with you.

Who only wants to be my friend.

I'll love you anyways,

even if it's a lonely fight.

Hold My Hand, Ease My Mind

Put your hand in mine.
I'm here for you.
Said, I love you.
Said I care.
You know that I want to be with you,
all the time.
Let me ease your mind.
Help you leave those lonely thoughts behind.
Take your time.
I don't care how long it takes.
For you to open your heart.
Don't be afraid to love again.
Those three words.
Sweet and simple.
Short and kind.

True and real.

Always kindle.

An aching heart to smile inside.

Our love,

I'll always treasure it.

Undying Affection

You came into my empty heart.
In some ways, I can't say no.
You broke down walls.
For your love to pass through.
I never resisted you in doing so.
You colored my heart red.
I never feared you.
You felt my warmth.
Let it be known.
A home of love in you,
I need.
The warmth from within,
isn't lust alone.
But a fire of my undying affection.
Burning with hope and faith.

Not a dramatic attraction.

But one true love,

that my heart always keeps.

Longer Than the Stars

Love to see you shine in the night.

Though I'm on the other side.

It's alright.

You say we're just friends.

No ones got to know what we do.

You've got your love locked up.

But I love you even at your worst.

Still put you first.

Because I know your worth.

So if you should know how long I'll love you.

I'd reply......

As long as the stars are above you.

And the sea is bound to wash upon the shore.

As long as I live through you.

As long as you want me to.

And longer by far.

Dreaming of You

At night I dream of us.
Our bodies entangled in bed.
I can still taste your kiss.
Feel your breath on my skin.
The touch of my hands,
sliding down your body.
As you whisper my name.
Longing to feel my strength in you.
I wish we were in the flesh.
Just let me dream.
Unless you're lying here beside me.
Reliving them instead.
Because these are not moments,
that I wish to miss.

Finding the Light

Don't worry about me.

Nor be concerned.

I knew it was a challenge.

Yet so much I learned.

I'm going to be alright.

We're not saying goodbye.

So I'm not going to cry.

But if I happen to.

I know I'll see your reflection in each teardrop.

I'm going to be alright.

I just hope you find your way.

Out of the darkness that surrounds you.

And find your way into the light.

Forever Grateful for You

I'll never forget the day we started talking.

Because that day I met my best friend.

Somebody that I want to have in my life,

forever.

And I'll forever be grateful for that day.

Because I met you.

For all this searching you're the best thing that I've found.

I don't always find the words to say.

But I think about you constantly.

Whether it's on my mind.

Or in my heart.

And it assures me that I'm never alone.

Beautifully Broken

I'm not trying to fix you.

I can't heal you.

I'm just trying to show you.

How beautiful your broken is.

Each piece fits into a masterpiece.

Of who you are now.

Right now, I see a beautiful soul.

You love deeply.

You've given people all of your light.

You want others to think you can't be hurt.

But the truth is......

You hurt easier than most.

Even though you're fierce and tender.

Within the same breath.

This is your beauty.

Therefore sweet contentment and all things of soulful beauty,

will always find you.

Love Across the Miles

Staring at the glow of the moon.

At the stars in the night sky,

I wonder.

An ocean apart from my town tonight.

As I hope you hear this cry from this heart of mine.

I feel you,

just not in my arms a thousand miles away.

But I feel your heart,

beating for us.

I hope you see my love all around you.

Amidst this pain.

But I feel you in my hands,

but you're not with me.

With all these words,

in my heart.

I see it in the sky,

the sun.

All of the day,

I want to be where you are.

But there's no place so far,

that my love can't reach.

Memories and Moments

Just as sand sifts through an hourglass.
Our time together drifts away from us,
to become only memories.
When I see your beautiful face.
Everything on my mind is erased.
Then I go to that special place,
where it's only you and I.
Hand in hand.
In deep green forests.
On shores of sand.
I'd even write your name in the sky, but why?
When a cloud would remove that.
I'd write your name in the sand,
but the wind would blow it away.
I'd write it in my heart so nothing could remove it.

And when memories are all that's left.

In my heart you will be,

moving forward.

You with me or me with you.

And in heaven to,

you shall have my hand.

Forever in Love: A Promise to Keep

All this time that you've been waiting.

You don't have to wait any more.

Here in my arms is where you should be.

Because your love makes me believe.

No ocean or mountain can keep us apart.

I'm giving you my heart forever.

Every breath I take,

I take for you and me.

That's a promise I'll keep.

Love like ours is hard to find.

I can't keep you off my mind.

Every night I think of you.

Under stars twinkling high above.

I know that there's a million stars between us.

You make me complete.

This love I feel is so strong.

With you my heart found home.

I know we'll be together forever.

Loving you faithfully.

You're my angel.

You've given me wings.

And if there's one thing in this world that I know is true.

It's the love that I feel when I'm thinking of you.

My love for you has no beginning.

Or end.

But between remembering and forgetting.

It could be hurt or crushed.

Or blown away and suffer in silence.

But it lies within your heart with understanding.

With that kind of love for you.

I feel wonderful.

Even if I shed tears.

Time seems wasted.

The silence betrayed or distance forgotten.

Feel my love within your heart,

with understanding.

That way regardless of how far you are.

You'll know it's true.

It's real.

Sweet Surrender: A Vow of Forever Love

Let me hold you and vow to be yours forever.
I'll give you my love with sweet surrender.
Because I've always wanted to love you.
Our hearts will beat as one.
As I see a pure and simple honesty in your eyes.
Your smile is one of the best smiles,
I've ever seen.
And it has captivated me since day one.
So let's not waste this time.
Let me fill your life with pleasure.
And make memories to treasure.
When the morning sun appears.
We'll find our way together.
We'll make it last forever.

So if you want to know how much I really love you.

Put your hand above my chest,

and feel it.

Left Without Answers

I love you.

Have high hopes for you.

But you left.

Without telling me why.

Taking your love.

Which kept my passions burning high.

My heart is wounded.

In silence it hides.

I still love you.

If you should ask.

I still have high hopes which I hold onto.

I still have dreams left for us to carry on.

All isn't gone.

My bleeding heart hasn't drowned everything.

Though the pain suffocates my soul.

I wonder if my heart truly knows,

the meaning of love at all?

Unpredictable Emotion

I thought that I understood the morals,
of this wide world.
I even learned the basics of how to follow,
where today is headed.
But there's a part of me,
who just can't find a name.
To give this unpredictable emotion.
You made unclear the distinction,
between what's inside and outside my heart.
Just fix your gaze upon my everything.
Because I want to show you the kind of days,
that would make anyone jealous.
Everything from here on out,
will be another chance for love.
Our tears and dreams can't be hidden,

within a fake smile.

Until now, I've never even known the pain of losing something.

I'm unable to bear getting hurt,

even though I don't want you to leave.

This feeling of being afraid to chase after you.....

is a first for me.

If I just remain my beautiful self,

I could finally grow up.

I learned this mistaken idea of strength from you.

I want to exchange sweet words with you.

These kinds of days that would surely make anyone jealous are out there.

Waiting for us.

Feel free to follow me on my writing career and journey

.' I'll Entertain Your Imagination, With Words'

Linkedin: robersonsr.ernest

Twitter: @thewriter1976

Instagram: ernest-roberson-sr

Facebook: Ernest Roberson Sr.

Amazon: amazon.com/author/ernestrobersonsr

Trient Press:trientpress.com/our-authors

www.ingramcontent.com/pod-product-compliance
Lightning Source LLC
Chambersburg PA
CBHW010140030826
48979CB00024B/1083
* 9 7 9 8 8 8 9 9 0 0 1 0 8 *